ZONDERVAN

Larryboy and the Sinister Snow Day

Copyright © 2003 by Big Idea, Inc. VEGGIETALES®, character names, likenesses and other indicia are trademarks of Big Idea, Inc. All rights reserved.

Requests for information should be addressed to:

Zonderkidz, *Grand Rapids, Michigan 49530*

ISBN 978-0-310-70561-1

Written by: *Sean Graffney*
Editors: *Cindy Kenney, Gwen Ellis*
Cover and Interior Illustrations: *Michael Moore*
Cover Design and Art Direction: *Big Idea Design*

Interior Design: *Big Idea Design and Holli Leegwater*

Printed in the United States of America

VeggieTales

LarryBoy

AND THE SINISTER SNOW DAY

WRITTEN BY
SEAN GAFFNEY

ILLUSTRATED BY
MICHAEL MOORE

BASED ON THE HIT VIDEO SERIES: LARRYBOY
CREATED BY PHIL VISCHER
SERIES ADAPTED BY TOM BANCROFT

ZONDER**kidz**

ZONDERVAN.com/
AUTHORTRACKER
follow your favorite authors

TABLE OF CONTENTS

CHAPTER 1

BUMBLING IN THE BUMBLE BASEMENT

It was very dark. In fact, it was impossible to see anything at all.

"Ouch!" cried a voice.

"Who's there?" asked a second, squeaky voice.

"It's me," replied the first voice. "Who said, 'Who's there?'"

"I did," said the second voice, getting squeakier.

"What are *you* doing here?" demanded the first voice.

"What are *you* doing here?" squeaked the second.

"I asked first," the first voice insisted. "Ouch, I stepped on something hard!"

"That's me!" the second voice squeaked in pain.

"What's going on here?" cried Bob, as suddenly the lights were turned on.

Bob, the editor of the *Daily Bumble,* stood near the light switch of the newspaper's printing room. Herbert and Wally looked up from the middle of the room where they were standing next to the large printing press. They both looked sheepish.

"What did you find, boss?" asked Vicki, the

Bumble's photographer. She bounded into the room behind Bob. Just then Larry, the newspaper's janitor, peeked into the room, too.

"What's going on?" asked Larry.

"Bob heard intruders in the print room," answered Vicki.

"Intruders!" Larry exclaimed. "This is a job for...excuse me, please."

Larry turned and dashed away. Bob and Vicki watched the janitor for a moment and then looked at each other and shrugged. Larry often acted strangely, and they were becoming used to it. They turned their attention back to Herbert and Wally.

"What are you two doing in my printing-press room?" asked Bob.

"Well..." said Wally.

"Well, what?" demanded Bob.

"I was going to change the headline for tomorrow's sports page," confessed Wally.

"Change it?" asked Bob. "What's wrong with 'Bumblyburg Baseball Has Bats in Its Belfry'?"

"Nothing," said Wally. "I just thought a better headline might say, 'Wally Beats Herbert in Bowling' instead."

"Now why didn't we think of that," sighed Vicki, rolling her eyes.

"What about you?" Bob asked Herbert.

"I was going to change the headline to read, 'Wally Snores,'" said Herbert.

Bob sighed. "When are the two of you ever going to learn?"

"What do you mean?" asked Wally. "We already graduated from school."

"I got straight A's in finger painting," said Herbert. "And that's not easy for a vegetable with no fingers."

"That's not what I mean," said Bob. "You keep letting your petty squabbles get you into trouble."

"What's a 'squabble'?" asked Herbert.

"It's a board game," replied Wally.

"That's Scrabble," said Vicki.

"Oh," said Wally.

"Have no fear, Larryboy is here!" said a voice from the doorway.

Bob, Vicki, Herbert, and Wally turned toward the door and saw...

CHAPTER 2

LARRYBOY TO THE RESCUE!

Larryboy! Supercucumber champion among vegetables, the green guardian of Bumblyburg, and an all-around nice guy!

"Step aside, Bob. I'll take care of these intimidating intruders," announced Larryboy.

"I don't think that will be necessary," said Bob. "These two are..."

But before Bob could finish his sentence, Larryboy leaped over and pushed him aside. Bob stumbled into the control panel of the printing press, and the machine roared to life.

"Don't try to run!" Larryboy yelled at the motionless Herbert and Wally.

"Okay," said Wally. Herbert just nodded.

"Villains always try to run," Larryboy whispered to Vicki. "But I'm too smart for that. Watch!"

POP! Larryboy shot off one of his plunger ears. The suction cup whizzed past the two intruders and wedged into the printing press.

"Hmm," mused Larryboy. "If they had been running, that shot

would have been a direct hit."

"But they aren't running," Vicki noted.

"Really?" asked Larryboy. "Hey, cut that out!"

"Cut what out?" asked Vicki.

"Someone's pulling on my plunger ear," said Larryboy.

Vicki looked at Bob, who looked at Wally, who looked at Herbert. No one was pulling either of Larryboy's plunger ears.

"No one is pulling either of your plunger ears," said Vicki. "But look at the printing press!"

Everyone looked at the spot where Larryboy's ear hit the machine. The plunger ear was being pulled inside the press, dragging Larryboy along with it!

"Help!" shouted Larryboy frantically, as he was being pulled closer to the press.

"Turn the machine off!" shouted Vicki. Larryboy was getting closer still.

"I'm trying!" shouted Bob. Larryboy was now pressed against the machine.

"Too late!" shouted Wally, as Larryboy disappeared into the press.

"I want to shout something too!" shouted Herbert, feeling left out.

It was indeed too late. Larryboy had been pulled into the printing press. Bob, Vicki, Herbert, and Wally looked on helplessly. The machine groaned.

"Ouch," winced Bob. "That's *got* to hurt."

CLANK! CLUNK! SPLAT! The machine continued making odd noises.

"Look, he's up there!" Wally exclaimed.

Larryboy briefly appeared near the top of the printing press.

"I'm OK," Larryboy said, before being pulled back into the machine.

"Yes, but is the printing press OK?" asked Bob. As if in answer, ink began spurting out the sides of the press.

"Oh, no," moaned Bob.

CLANK! CLUNK! SPLAT! And then suddenly a final **SPLOOSH!** Larryboy shot out of the end of the machine. He was bundled with a stack of newspapers, and the headline "School Back in Session" was printed across his forehead.

"Are you all right?" asked Vicki.

"Sure," said Larryboy. He was acting tough to impress Vicki.

"That's one way to get your uniform pressed," she joked.

"Now we're going to have to reset the whole thing," said Bob. "It's going to be a late night."

"Sorry," said Larryboy.

"Don't feel sorry for us," said Vicki. "You should feel sorry for Larry, our janitor."

"Meeee?" squealed Larryboy. "I mean, *me* feel sorry for Larry? Why should I feel sorry for Larry?"

"Look at this place," said Vicki. The room was a mess. Ink was splattered everywhere—on the walls, on the ceiling, even on Bob. "It's going to take Larry days to clean up this room."

"Ulp," said Larryboy.

"Come on, Vicki," said Bob. "We have a paper to put out."

CHAPTER 3

WHETHER THE WEATHER IS SUNNY OR NOT

WHAP!

A newspaper bounced against the door of the Asparagus' house. The door flew open as Junior dashed out, snatched up the paper, and ran back inside. He raced to the living room, plopped down on the floor, and opened it up. Junior quickly flipped past the book review of Chief Croswell's best-seller, *Littering, Loitering, and the Law.* He barely saw the photo of Herbert and Wally breaking the world eating record as they devoured a sixty-foot-tall leaning tower of pizza. He found the page he was looking for and eagerly scanned it.

"Rats!" Junior grumbled, as his dad came around the corner.

"What's wrong, Son?" he asked.

"It's the weather report," said Junior. "I was hoping for a snowstorm this morning."

"A snowstorm in *September?*" Junior's dad chuckled. "That would be surprising. But don't worry. It will snow in a couple of months."

"A couple of months?" Junior yelped. "But

that's a lifetime away! I want it to snow today."

"But if it snowed today," his dad reasoned, "they might have to cancel school. You wouldn't want that, would you?"

Junior's dad had missed the point completely. That is exactly *why* Junior wanted it to snow!

"Dad," said Junior, "you completely missed the point. That is exactly why I want it to snow!"

"I thought you liked school," he said.

"Sure, when I was a *kid*," said Junior. "But now that I'm growing up, I have better things to do."

"Growing up? But you *are* still in grade school," said Dad.

"The way I see it," said Junior, "counting preschool, I've already had several years of classes. So I'm basically nearing adulthood!"

Dad chuckled and picked the paper up from the floor. "Really?" he said. "Well, just remember that God wants everyone to keep learning. Even grown-ups! When you stop learning, you stop growing."

"Sure, Dad," Junior said. "Can I look at the paper again?"

"Of course. What are you looking for?"

"I forgot to see if it's going to snow *tomorrow*," said Junior.

"It's not going to snow tomorrow," his dad replied.

"Too bad," moaned Junior, as he stared out the window at the clouds and dreamed of snow.

CHAPTER 4

MEANWHILE, OUTSIDE THE WINDOW...

A dangerous-looking snow pea named Avalanche crouched in the bushes outside the Asparagus home. He positioned a large microphone right next to the window. Then he ran a thick wire from the microphone out to the street.

Parked on the street was a white van with tinted windows. It read Unmarked Van Rental—When You Need to Not Be Noticed. Dozens of thick wires ran from the neighborhood houses to the van. Avalanche quickly hopped inside with his wire, slamming the door behind him.

Inside the van sat two other snow peas, the aggressive Frostbite and the oversized (but somewhat dim) Snowflake. Avalanche plugged the wire into the side of a large radio console that filled the back of the van. Frostbite put on a pair of headphones.

"It's a little asparagus kid," Frostbite said. "He's telling his dad that he hopes it snows."

"Ooh," said Snowflake. "I like snow."

"He's just like every other kid on the block," Frostbite said. "They all want a snow day, so they won't have to go to school."

"Gee," said Snowflake. "I liked school."

"You did *not*," said Avalanche.

"Sure I did," Snowflake insisted. "Why do you think I spent five years in first grade?"

"Quiet, you two," said Frostbite. "The leader is calling in."

Frostbite hit a button on the console. A menacing voice cackled over the loudspeaker.

"Good work, gentlemen," said the gravelly voice. "I have been monitoring the transmissions from the microphones you set up."

"Thank you, sir," said Frostbite. "All the children want a snow day."

"Of course they do," intoned the voice. "And soon I will use that desire to trick the children into helping us. And when they do, we will turn all of Bumblyburg into a frozen wasteland! Bwaa-haaa-haaa!"

The evil laugh echoed in the van.

"BWAA-HAAA-HAAA!" laughed Frostbite.

"BWAA-HAAA-HAAA!" laughed Avalanche.

"BWAA-HAAA-HAAA?" said Snowflake. "I don't get it."

Snowflake often didn't get it. So he did what he always did when he didn't get it: he pulled out a comic book and waited for the others to stop laughing.

CHAPTER 5

OH, THOSE GOLDEN-RULE DAYS

The auditorium was packed with superheroes, all craning their necks to see the stage.
A hush fell over the crowd as Bok Choy, the wise
professor, stepped up to the podium.

"Superheroes and superheroes-in-training," Bok
Choy began, "you are all gathered here this day to
witness an event that has never happened before in
our school. We are giving a diploma to a trainee
before he finishes all of his classes!"

The crowd erupted in cheers. Some of the heroes
began to chant, **"LARRYBOY! LARRYBOY!"**

Bok Choy called for quiet.

"That's right," the professor said. "Larryboy is so
naturally gifted, so scholastically stupendous, so
downright super, he doesn't need to attend classes
anymore. There is nothing more for him to learn!"

The crowd once again began their chant.
Larryboy, urged on by the crowd, made his
way toward the stage. Bok Choy handed
him a diploma, which Larryboy graciously
accepted.

"Thank you, fellow superheroes. It is a great privilege..."
he began, but someone was interrupting. Larryboy
scanned the crowd for this unwanted intruder.

"Larryboy, wake up!"

"Aw, peanut brittle," he mumbled, as he awoke from
his dream.

LET'S TRY THAT AGAIN—

THE REAL CHAPTER FIVE...
NOT THE DREAM

Larryboy was sitting at his
desk in class. He was taking 'Superhero
101: The Basics of Being Super' at the
Bumblyburg Community College. The drowsy
cucumber could see Bok Choy lecturing at the
front of the room. His classmate, Scarlet Tomato,
leaned closer.

"Larryboy," Scarlet whispered, "wake up!"

"I'm awake," Larryboy insisted. "In fact, I wasn't
sleeping at all."

"Yes, you were," said the red heroine. "You were
snoring."

"Was not," Larryboy replied.

"Were to."

"I wasn't snoring," Larryboy said, trying to think
fast. "I was practicing Morse code. With snorts."

"Really?" asked Scarlet Tomato.

"Yep. Pretty good, huh? **SNORT! SNORT! SNORT!**"
Larryboy made an obnoxious noise through his
nose. "That, my friend, is the letter *s.*"

Scarlet Tomato looked at Larryboy with
disbelief.

23

"Okay, I was sleeping. I'm sorry," Larryboy confessed.

"Well, sleeping or practicing, you've missed the lecture."

That much was true. Bok Choy was just finishing.

"And that," he concluded, "is how I defeated the Snow King! Class dismissed."

The superheroes packed up their books and headed out.

"Except," called Bok Choy, "for Larryboy."

"Oops," said Larryboy.

"Tough break," Lemon Twist called out. The other heroes just giggled. Larryboy walked to the front of the classroom.

"Yes, Professor Choy?" Larryboy asked.

Bok Choy looked meaningfully at the young hero. Larryboy was too embarrassed to look his teacher in the eye.

"Were you sleeping in my class?" asked Bok Choy.

"No, of course not. Don't be silly. Well, maybe a little."

"Son, someday you will realize how important an education is," the teacher said. "When that day comes, you will wish you hadn't slept through so many lectures."

"Yes, sir," said Larryboy.

"You can go."

"Thank you, Professor Choy," said Larryboy. The embarrassed cucumber hurried out of the room.

CHAPTER 6

THE RIDE HOME

VROOOM! Larryboy raced his Larrymobile toward home. Suddenly, his videophone chirped. Archibald, Larryboy's butler, appeared on the video screen.

"Good evening, Master Larry," said Archibald.

"Hello, Archie," muttered the cucumber.

"And how was class this evening?" asked his butler.

"Class?" said Larryboy. "Stimulating. Invigorating. Awe-inspiring."

"Oh?" asked Archibald. "So you fell asleep again?"

"Maybe," Larryboy admitted. "But it wasn't my fault. The lecture was really boring. In fact, school is boring."

"But school can be so much fun," said Archibald. "There are so many good things to learn. I love attending classes."

"I don't," said Larryboy. "I'm an accomplished superhero. I know so much already, I don't need any more schooling. Besides, I have more important things to do with my time."

"Like what?"

"Like playing Tic-Tac-Toe on our Larrycomputer," said Larryboy. "Tonight, I think I can win!"

Archibald sighed as Larryboy clicked off the videophone. "And when it comes to trying to teach you something, Master Larry, it seems *I* can never win."

CHAPTER 7

THE ICE PLOT THICKENS

"After all, I'm a mature elementary-school kid; I have no more need for schooling." Junior Asparagus stood in the middle of the clubhouse to make his announcement. Laura Carrot, Percy Pea, and Renee Blueberry applauded.

"Me too," said Laura. "I'm sure I've learned all there is to know, at least all that I *need* to know."

"Me too," said Percy. "I've learnt lots."

"That's 'learned,'" corrected Laura.

"I already know how to speak French and English," said Renee, an exchange student from France. She liked to remind others that she was bilingual. "That's more than some teachers."

"And I know both English and Pig Latin," Percy offered.

"Pig Latin isn't a real language," said Renee.

"It-tay is-say ooh-tay," Percy replied.

"We should make a pact," said Junior. "No more school."

"Oui," agreed Renee.

"Yes," said Percy.

"Yeah," Laura chimed in. "Except…"

"Except what?"

Everyone turned to look at Laura.

"Except," she said, "won't we get into trouble?"

"Oh, right," said Junior. "I hadn't thought about that. Does anybody have any other ideas?"

Suddenly there was a knock at the clubhouse door.

"Come in," said Junior.

The door opened. The three snow peas—Avalanche, Frostbite, and Snowflake—stepped into the clubhouse.

"Hello," said one of the snow peas. "My name is Frostbite. These are my brothers, Avalanche and Snowflake."

"Hello," said Junior.

"We aren't supposed to talk with strangers," said Laura.

"Oh, OK," said Snowflake. He turned and walked toward the door, but Avalanche stopped him.

"We'll be going," said Frostbite. "But first, we wanted to tell you kids something."

"What's that?" asked Junior.

"Yeah, what's that?" asked Snowflake.

"We couldn't help overhearing what you were talking about," said Frostbite. "About not wanting to go to school."

"Yeah," said Avalanche. "We heard you wished there was a way to get out of going to school without getting into trouble."

"We tried to be polite and not listen," said Snowflake. "But it was hard not to hear while we were crouching outside your window."

Avalanche gave Snowflake a sharp nudge.

"Ow!" said the snow pea. "What was that for?"

"Anyway," said Frostbite, quickly changing the subject, "what if we told you that there *is* a way to get out of going to school without getting into trouble? What would you say to that?"

"Wow," said Percy. "For real?"

"No school and no trouble?" asked Laura suspiciously. "I don't believe it."

"Believe it," said Avalanche. "In fact, your parents will be the ones to tell you to stay home."

"No way!" whispered Junior. "But how?"

"You want a snow day, right?" asked Frostbite, mischievously. "Well, we know how you can create your own snow day. And you don't have to wait for winter."

"All you have to do," said Avalanche, "is promise not to tell anyone about it."

The kids looked at each other.

"What do you think, Junior?" asked Renee.

"I don't know," said Junior, looking quite concerned. "It sounds too good to be true."

"But it couldn't hurt to listen to their idea, could it?" asked Percy hopefully.

"Come on, Junior," said Laura, nudging her friend. "A *snow* day. In September."

"OK," said Junior. "We'll listen. But no promises."

"Of course not," said Frostbite. "Now gather around. And remember, it's a *secret*."

The kids formed a tight circle around Frostbite. They oohed and aahed as they heard the plan—except for Snowflake, who still didn't get it.

CHAPTER 8

BACK AT THE BUMBLE

"Is it dangerous?" Vicki asked. She stood in front of Bob's desk in the editor's office of the *Daily Bumble*.

"It's not dangerous," Bob said. "But it *is* an important assignment, Vicki."

"I was hoping for a dangerous assignment," said Vicki. "All my latest assignments have been a little boring."

"If my information is correct," said the editor, "Bumblyburg won't be boring for long."

Just then there was a knock at the door. Larry, the janitor, stuck his head in.

"Excuse me," said Larry. "I need to clean the ceiling tiles."

"If you have to," said Bob.

Larry entered the room. He attached a squeegee to the end of a long pole and began to wipe the ceiling tiles. Water dripped from his squeegee onto Bob's desk.

"As I was saying," Bob continued, frantically moving his papers this way and that—to avoid the drips. "There is a new supervillain on the loose. His name is Iceberg."

"Iceberg! Really?" asked Larry.

"Really," said Bob, as a drop of water splattered onto his head. "Could you be a little more careful with that squeegee?"

"Sure," said Larry.

"I've heard of him," said Vicki. "His dad was a supervillain back in the days when Bok Choy protected Bumblyburg."

"That's right," said Bob. "Iceberg has been causing trouble with his love of all things cold. He disrupted the big game at the Salad Bowl by creating a hailstorm. And in South Pimento, he froze the mayor's duck pond, turning it into a skating rink!"

"Those poor ducks," sighed Vicki.

"No kidding," said Bob. "Can you imagine how hard it was to find skates that fit webbed feet?"

"So, what's Iceberg up to now?" asked the photographer.

"There is a rumor," said Bob, "that he plans to hit Bumblyburg next!"

"That *is* a big story," said Vicki. "I'm on it!"

Larry was hanging on to every word. In fact he was listening so carefully that he wasn't watching where he was washing. Before he knew it, the ceiling fan snagged his squeegee, and he was lifted into the air!

"Help!" shouted Larry, as he circled the room.

"Look out!" shouted Vicki, as she ducked in rhythm with the fan blades

"Get down from there!" shouted Bob.

But Larry only spun around faster and faster. He knocked over the books on Bob's bookshelf. He knocked over Bob's lamp. Then he knocked over Bob!

"Ouch," moaned Bob. "Larry!"

"Sorry," said Larry.

CLICK! Larry's spinning slowed to a stop. Vicki had turned off the fan.

"You OK, Boss?" she asked Bob.

"Yeah," Bob said. "Although I can't say the same for our janitor."

Vicki turned toward Larry, who was still clinging to the fan, suspended in midair. The janitor giggled.

"I haven't been this dizzy since I put my overalls in the washer," he said.

"Why would that make you dizzy?" asked Vicki.

"I was still wearing them."

"Are you going to come down from there?" asked Bob.

"I don't know," said Larry. "Are you mad?"

"Yes," said Bob.

"Then I think I'll stay up here awhile."

"Suit yourself," said Bob.

"I'll leave you two alone," said Vicki, quickly leaving the room.

CHAPTER 9

TROUBLE UNDERFOOT WHEN IT RAINS

CLUNK!

Frostbite had just attached a huge metal cylinder to the ceiling of the sewer pipe. He could reach the ceiling because he was standing on top of Avalanche, who was standing on top of Snowflake.

"There. That's the last Mini-Hooha we needed to put into place," Frostbite announced.

"What are Mini-Hoohas anyway?" asked Snowflake.

"These metal gadgets we have been attaching to the ceiling. What do you think?" asked Frostbite. "Now set us down."

Snowflake looked up at the ceiling to study the large cylinder.

"You're leaning back too far!" shouted Frostbite.

"Be careful!" demanded Avalanche.

The two snow peas were leaning perilously to the left. Snowflake shifted his weight. Now his two friends were leaning perilously to the right. Snowflake shifted again.

SPLASH! All three tumbled into the messy

sewer water.

"Yuck!" cried the peas.

"I just spent the whole day putting these gadgets into place," groaned Frostbite, "and now I'm tired and wet. Thanks a lot!"

"Yeah, I was meaning to ask about that," said Snowflake. "Why did we put all these Mini-Hoohas in the sewer under the streets of Bumblyburg anyway?"

"Listen, freeze brain," said Frostbite, not so nicely. "Each Mini-Hooha is attached to the boss's K.w.a.c.k. machine by these pipes. So when the boss throws the switch, the K.w.a.c.k. will fill up each Mini-Hooha with F.r.i.s.b.e.e.s. Got it?"

"Got it," said Snowflake, but his face revealed that he really didn't.

"Don't worry, Snowflake," said Avalanche. "You'll understand soon enough. That is, if the kids do their part."

"Yeah," said Frostbite. "It's up to the kids now."

...AND RAINS

It was almost midnight. Junior was lying in his bed, staring at the clock. As the second hand approached twelve, he whispered, "Five, four, three, two, one!" Junior jumped out of bed and ran to the door of his bedroom. He carefully pulled the door open and listened. No sounds could be heard from the hallway.

"I sure hope Mom and Dad are asleep," he whispered to himself.

Junior snuck out the door and hopped quietly down

the hall, stopping outside his parents' room to listen.

SNORT.

The loud sound made Junior jump. Were his parents awake?

SHOOOO.

Junior continued to listen.

SNORT. SHOOOO. SNORT. SHOOOO. SNORT. SHOOOO.

It was the sound of snoring! Junior sighed in relief; his parents were definitely asleep. Junior continued down the hall and into the bathroom, quietly closing the door behind him.

"First, the tub," Junior said to himself.

He moved to the tub and put the stopper into the drain. Then he turned on the water. Next, Junior moved to the sink. He put a stopper into the sink drain and turned on the water there too. Quickly hopping back to the door, he opened it and listened.

The only sound was a not-so-soft snoring coming from his parents' room. Junior swiftly moved down the hall and ducked back into his bedroom. He closed his door and hopped into bed.

"Whew!" he sighed. "I wonder how the others are doing?"

...AND RAINS

Down the street from Junior's house, a similar scene was being played out. Laura had just turned on the water at her kitchen sink, when her brother peeked around the corner.

"I got the bathtub going," said Lenny.

"Good job," said Laura.

Then they headed back upstairs.

...AND POURS

Percy Pea lived right around the corner from Laura Carrot. Returning from his bathroom, he hopped back into bed. Then he looked out the window just in time to see the sprinklers on his neighbor's lawn come on. He could see Renee Blueberry as she dashed from the lawn back to her front door. Percy smiled and snuggled down into his bed as he thought about all his other friends turning on the faucets in the neighborhood, too. Everything was going according to plan.

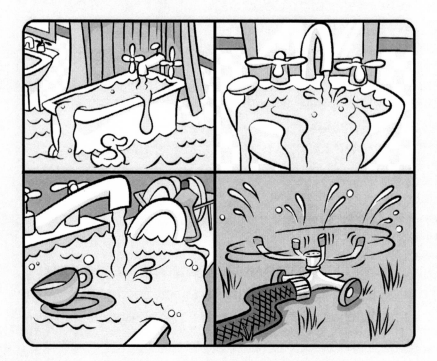

CHAPTER 10

WHERE'S AN ARK WHEN YOU NEED ONE?

Early the next morning, Archibald gently
nudged Larry, who was in bed, fast asleep. He
was snoring loudly.

"Master Larry," said Archibald. "Please wake up."

"I know the answer," he shouted as he sat up. "I
wasn't sleeping!"

"Master Larry, it's me," said Archibald.

"Archie," said Larry. "Why didn't you say so? I
thought I was in trouble again."

"You aren't in trouble," assured his butler. "But
Bumblyburg *is*. And they need a superhero, right now!"

"They do?" said Larry, getting excited.
"I...am...that...hero!"

"Yes, you are," Archibald agreed.

He held out the Larryboy suit, freshly cleaned
and ironed, as Larry hopped out of bed and dashed
behind the changing screen.

"What seems to be the trouble?" he asked.

"During the night, someone turned on
every faucet in Bumblyburg. The whole
town is flooded."

"Oh," Larry said, poking

his head around the corner. "Then Bumblyburg doesn't really need a superhero. It sounds like it needs a plumber."

"Perhaps," Archibald admitted. "*If* this was an accident. But Police Chief Croswell suspects foul play."

"Ah, yes," said Larryboy. "This sounds just like the work of 'foul play.'" Larryboy nodded wisely.

Archibald waited, knowing the question would come.

"Who is 'foul play'?" asked Larryboy.

"Perhaps if you would pay more attention in class," said Archibald, "you would know that 'foul play' isn't a person. It means 'an evil plot.'"

"I knew that," said Larry, disappearing behind the screen again.

"Chief Croswell thinks that a supervillain might be attacking Bumblyburg," Archibald went on. "It could be another one of Awful Alvin's schemes or even Plumb Loco."

"Or maybe that ice cube guy that they were talking about at the *Daily Bumble*," suggested Larry.

"Iceberg," corrected Archibald. "Maybe."

"It doesn't matter," said Larry. "None of them is a match for..." Larry jumped out from behind the screen in full uniform. "Larryboy!" he announced.

"Exactly," said Archibald. "And except for the fact that you put your uniform on over your pajamas, you are all set to go."

"Right," said Larryboy, disappearing behind the screen again.

CHAPTER 11

THE ICEBERG COMETH

ZOOM!

Larryboy flew over Bumblyburg in the Larryplane. The whole town was indeed flooded, covered knee-deep in water. Well, knee-deep for average-sized citizens, like cucumbers and carrots. For shorter vegetables, like tomatoes and peppers, it was a whole lot deeper. And for tall Bumblyburgians like celery, it wasn't as deep. You get the idea.

"Look! There's Officer Olaf," said Larryboy.

Larryboy sent the plane into a dive toward the street. As the Larryplane neared the ground, the wings tucked into the sides of the plane and the wheels popped out. The Larryplane was transformed into the Larrymobile!

SPLASH! The Larrymobile hit the road, splattering water everywhere. Our hero splashed up to Officer Olaf's squad car, sitting in the middle of the road.

"Hey, Olaf!" Larry called.

Officer Olaf rolled down his window.

"Larryboy, am I glad to see you," said the policeman. "The whole town of Bumblyburg is

flooded. The streets are a mess, and panic is setting in. People are getting soaked just going out to pick up the morning paper. And on top of that, the morning papers are all soggy!"

"I see," said Larryboy.

"And now, even I'm stuck. My engine is flooded!"

"Well," said Larryboy, "you should expect that when driving in a flood. Kind of silly, don't you think?"

Just then the engine of the Larrymobile sputtered and died.

"Oops," said our hero. "Sure wish I could get to the Larryspeedboat!"

"Looks like we are both stuck until the flood subsides," said Olaf.

"How long will that be?" asked Larryboy.

"It will take days for the water to drain off."

"It will take longer than that!" A strange voice boomed

across the waters. Larryboy and Olaf looked up and noticed a van parked directly across the street. The side door of the van was open. Inside the van was a large, clear plastic bowl. And sitting in the bowl was...

"Eek! A large head!" screamed Larryboy. "Of lettuce!"

"Looks like the picture of Iceberg on *Bumblyburg's Most Wanted*," said Olaf.

"That's right," boomed the voice of the lettuce head. "I am Iceberg, and I'm the new master of the soon-to-be-icy Bumblyburg!"

"Get him, Larryboy!" shouted Olaf.

"OK!" shouted Larryboy. "Prepare to meet your match, Iceberg!" Larryboy reached for his door handle.

"It's too late," laughed Iceberg.

And as he laughed, the streets of Bumblyburg began to shake.

CHAPTER 12

ICE CAPADES

"What's happening?" Officer Olaf had to shout to be heard over the loud rumbling.

"What?" shouted Larryboy. "I can't hear you. You will have to shout to be heard over the loud rumbling."

"I said," shouted Olaf, "what's happening?"

"I am happening," boomed Iceberg. **"BWAA-HAAA-HAAAA!"**

"Hey, I recognize that laugh," said Larryboy. "That is the universal 'evil-menace-to-society' laugh. Only supervillains use that laugh!"

"That's right," Iceberg agreed. "Even now, my machinery is transforming the flood waters of Bumblyburg."

"You're getting rid of the water?" shouted Larryboy. "How thoughtful of you. And I thought you were going to be an evil menace!"

"Not getting rid of," teased Iceberg, "but transforming."

With a loud **CRACK!** the rumbling stopped.

"Glad that's over," said our hero. "Now to see about that head of lettuce."

"Yikes, my door is stuck," said Officer Olaf. "Larryboy, look at the water!"

Larryboy gasped. The water had turned to ice and the Larrymobile was stuck in it. In fact, *all* of Bumblyburg was stuck in ice!

"It worked!" Iceberg crowed. "My plan to turn Bumblyburg into a frozen wasteland has worked!"

"I'll get you for this," Larryboy warned.

"How?" asked the head. "You can't even get out of your car."

"My Larrymobile comes equipped with a special crime-fighting feature made especially for situations like this!"

"What's that?"

"A canopy!" Larryboy quickly popped open the canopy and hopped out onto the ice.

"Not so fast," Iceberg said. He then called out, "Boys!"

ZOOM! ZOOM! ZOOM!

Frostbite, Avalanche, and Snowflake jumped out of the van. Each wore a jet-skate! They zoomed across the ice and encircled Larryboy.

"Only three of you?" taunted Larryboy. "No problem. I can take on all three of you with my arms tied behind my back. If I had arms, that is." The super cucumber hopped toward Frostbite. But he promptly slipped on the ice and fell down.

"Nice try," taunted Frostbite.

"Oh, yeah?" Larryboy responded. He quickly leaped back up to a standing position—and just as quickly slid into a lying-down position.

"This is embarrassing," the cucumber moaned.

"Can't catch us if you can't even stand up," Avalanche teased.

"Oh, yeah?"

POP! Larryboy shot one of his plunger ears straight at Avalanche.

PLOP! It stuck to the snow pea!

"Who's laughing now?" asked our hero.

Avalanche zoomed away from Larryboy. The rope attached to the plunger ear became taut. **SWOOSH!** Just like a water-skier, Larryboy was pulled across the ice!

HMMM, thought Larryboy. **THIS ISN'T EXACTLY WHAT I HAD IN MIND.**

"Hey, fellows," shouted Avalanche. "Let's play whiplash!"

Frostbite and Snowflake glided over to Avalanche, hooked themselves together, and zoomed across the ice, with Larryboy in tow. Then they came to a sudden stop! Larryboy whipped past the trio.

"AAAAHHHH!" screamed Larryboy. Our hero continued sliding until he hit the wall of the Bumblyburg Library. Larryboy slid down the wall in a daze.

"That was fun," said Snowflake.

"Let's do it again!" suggested Avalanche.

"Yippee!" said Frostbite.

The three took off at high speed. Soon, the dazed Larryboy was skiing behind them again.

"Mommy."

"Larryboy!" shouted Officer Olaf. "Release the plunger!"

"What?" shouted Larryboy.

"Release the plunger!"

"Good idea," replied the hero. He turned his head to the side.

POP! The plunger popped off of Avalanche. But too late! The three had already stopped, and Larryboy whipped on past, heading straight for Iceberg's van!

"Look out!" shouted the cucumber.

CRASH! Larryboy flew through the van door and smacked into the wall.

"Hello, Larryboy. I appreciate your dropping by," the

villain said. "You don't look so good."

"Eep," said Larryboy.

"And to think I was afraid you would spoil my plans," laughed Iceberg.

"Eep," said Larryboy.

"Well, just to make sure you don't crack this ice capade, you can come and stay with me!" said Iceberg, as he slammed the door shut. Avalanche zoomed to the van and jumped into the driver's side. The engine revved to life, and the van zoomed across the ice.

"Hey, look!" shouted Olaf. "The van was really a rocket-sled in disguise!"

"Nice detective work," Frostbite teased Olaf, skating right up to the police cruiser.

"I hope you have learned something in all of this," the snow pea taunted.

"Learned something? Like what?" asked Officer Olaf.

"That *we* control Bumblyburg now. Come on, Snowflake!" Frostbite and Snowflake skated off, laughing.

"Hey, that's not funny," shouted Olaf. "Besides, I know Larryboy! He'll find a way to escape and make you all pay!"

The two villains had disappeared.

"At least, I think he will," added Olaf, not really as sure as he sounded.

CHAPTER 13

SNOW DAY

"Bumblyburg overcome by ice!"
Junior leaned into the radio as the
announcer continued the broadcast.
"Larryboy disappeared while battling
Iceberg and his henchmen," the announcer said.
"Police continue their search. In the meantime,
all vehicles are advised to stay off the roads.
This includes cars, mopeds, motorized pogo sticks,
and school buses. So until further notice, school is
canceled."

"Wahoo!" Junior flicked off the radio and ran to the
front hall. He threw on his coat, hat, and scarf, and
raced out the door. His sled was waiting on the porch,
where he had left it earlier. He had been pretty confi-
dent school would be canceled!

"Just when you thought a day couldn't get any
better!" Junior looked up at the falling snow. The
weather report had called for rain all morning, but
the extreme cold caused by the Bumblyburg ice
turned the rain into snow. The entire town was
blanketed in white.

The streets were full of kids. Some had

sleds, some ice skates. A snowman was already in progress on the corner. A snowball fight was brewing on the other end of the block.

"Hey, Junior!" Laura Carrot was waving from the street. Percy and Renee stood beside her. Laura pulled a toboggan. Percy and Renee each had snowboards.

"Hey, Laura."

"We're heading to Mortimer's Run. Want to come?" asked Percy.

"You bet," said Junior. The foursome headed up the hill.

"Pretty cool, the ice and all, huh?" asked Percy.

"And no one suspects a thing!" said Renee.

"I wonder," said Junior.

"About what?" asked Laura.

"Well, they say that Larryboy tried to stop Iceberg. Why would Larryboy do that, unless something was wrong?"

"What do you mean?" asked Percy. "We get a snow day, and no one got hurt. What could be wrong?"

"Nothing, I guess," agreed Junior.

"Let's race," said Laura. "Last one to the top of the hill is a rotten tomato!"

"Or a brown banana," chimed Renee.

"Or an apple when it gets those spots that are kind of mushy and..." Percy noticed that the others weren't listening. Instead, they were already speeding away.

"Hey, wait for me!" he cried.

Laughing, the children raced to the top of the hill.

CHAPTER 14

INTO EVERYONE'S LIFE
A LITTLE GLOATING MUST FALL

"That was so easy!" Iceberg sat in his bowl in the middle of his hideout. Frostbite, Avalanche, and Snowflake stood around him, listening.

"As slick as ice," said Frostbite.

"As smooth as snow," said Avalanche.

"As orange as my cat," said Snowflake.

The other villians stared at the snow pea in confusion.

"What? My cat is orange," explained Snowflake.

"Anyway," said Iceberg, with a scowl, "my plan took place without a hitch. The kids played their parts perfectly."

"What irony," said Frostbite. "Bumblyburg's own kids helped us out."

"And we skated circles around the local law enforcement," said Avalanche.

"Actually, I did more of a figure eight," said Snowflake.

"And Bumblyburg's superhero is just a superjoke," said Iceberg.

"I heard that!" said Larryboy. The cucumber sat forlorn in his ice cage.

"I wanted you to hear that," jeered the master villain.

"Well, you won't get away with this," said Larryboy.

"I already did," laughed Iceberg. "In fact, I accomplished what my father, the Snow King, could never do. I conquered Bumblyburg!"

"Yeah, well, you won't get away with this for much longer," said Larryboy. "I'm a trained superhero. We are taught to take care of villains like you."

"Oh, yeah?" replied Iceberg. "And just what did they teach you?"

"Stuff," said Larryboy. "I just don't remember it right now."

"Hah!" Iceberg gloated. "A superhero that doesn't pay attention in class."

"I don't need to pay attention in class," Larryboy retorted. "I don't need classes to defeat you."

"I wish you would be quiet," said Iceberg. "You're ruining my celebration party."

"I'll take care of him," said Frostbite. "Hey, pickle-boy."

"I'm not a pickle-boy," said Larryboy. "I'm a cucumber-boy."

"Whatever. I dare you to stick your tongue to the ice bar of your cage."

"That's silly," said Larryboy. "Why would I do that?"

"Are you chicken?" taunted Frostbite.

"No, I'm a cucumber," said Larryboy.

"Prove it," said Frostbite.

"OK," said Larryboy, sticking his tongue against the

bar. "Thee? No pwobwem."

But when Larryboy tried to pull his tongue back into his mouth, it was stuck!

"Hey," he said, "my thongue ith thtuck!"

Iceberg and the snow peas laughed.

"Dowen waff," lisped Larryboy. "Ith na thunny!"

But the villains laughed even louder because, to be honest, it *was* funny.

CHAPTER 15

MUCH LATER

"Wow, a whole week without school. This is great!" Junior said. He and his friends were on their way to the clubhouse.

"Yeah, a whole week of sledding," said Percy.

"It sure is fun," agreed Renee. "Isn't it?

"Of course it is," said Percy.

When they entered the clubhouse, Laura was already there, reading. But as her friends entered, Laura hid her book.

"What are you doing, Laura?" asked Junior.

"Nothing," she said.

"It looked like you were reading," said Renee.

"How was sledding?" asked Laura.

"Got it!" Percy shouted. He had sneaked behind Laura and was holding up her book. "A math book!"

"So I was reading a math book," said Laura. "So what?"

"So we aren't going to school all week," said Junior. "You don't have to look at math."

"What if I wanted to?"

"Why would you want to do *that*?" asked Renee.

"To me, math problems are like puzzles," said Laura. "And without school, well, I miss doing them. I guess I like math."

"I can't believe it," said Percy. "She misses *math!*"

"What's wrong with that?" demanded Laura.

"If you are going to miss anything," Percy teased, "it should be reading."

"You miss reading?" asked Junior.

"Don't you?" Percy responded. "I'm a pretty good reader. And there are lots of cool stories out there. I was kinda looking forward to reading another one."

"Someday, you will be reading *my* books," said Renee. "When I grow up, I'm going to be a famous author."

"For real?" asked Percy.

"For real," said Renee. "Of course, I still have to learn how to become a good writer."

"When I grow up, I'm going to be an engineer," said Junior.

"You'll need to know a lot of math to be an engineer," said Laura.

"I will?"

"Of course."

"Gee, what if Bumblyburg *stays* frozen and we don't *ever* get to go back to school? Then I'll never get to be an engineer," said Junior.

"And I'll never become a writer," said Renee.

"Maybe school wasn't so bad after all," suggested Junior.

"I miss art class too," said Laura. "Especially painting."

"I really liked gym class," said Percy.

There was a long pause. "I think we may have made a mistake," said Junior.

"Do you think so?" asked Percy.

"I do," said Junior. "My dad told me that when you stop learning, you stop growing. He said that God wants us to keep learning, even after we grow up. I think we have disappointed him. And maybe a whole lot of other people too."

"I think you're right, Junior," said Laura. "We never should have helped those snow peas."

"Now we'll never be able to go back to school!" cried Percy.

"What can we do?" asked Renee.

"There's only one thing we *can* do," said Junior. "We have to find Larryboy. Then he can help us make things right again."

CHAPTER 16

FOLLOW THAT VILLAIN!

"Can't catch me! Can't catch me!" Frostbite taunted Officer Olaf and Chief Croswell.

The two police officers tried to grab the villain as he skated around them on his jet-skate. But both officers had trouble keeping their balance on the ice. Frostbite came to a stop close to Olaf.

"Catch me high!" the snow pea taunted.

Officer Olaf grabbed for Frostbite, but the villain zoomed away too quickly. He skated near Croswell.

"Catch me low!" he yelled at the policeman.

Croswell reached out, but again Frostbite zoomed off before he could be nabbed. The snow pea came to a halt directly in between Olaf and Croswell.

"Catch me in the middle!" he shouted.

"I've got him!" yelled Olaf as he dove for Frostbite.

"No, I've got him!" yelled Croswell, jumping for Frostbite from the opposite direction. Croswell and Olaf almost reached Frostbite at the same time, but the snow pea zoomed away at the last second.

BAM!

Olaf and Croswell smashed into each other. They spun around on the ice, landing in a pile.

"Much too slow!" yelled Frostbite. Laughing, he zoomed away.

"Look, there goes Frostbite," whispered Junior to Laura, Percy, and Renee. The four of them were at the top of a hill, looking down on the streets.

"Larryboy was last seen with Iceberg and the snow peas," he continued. "If we follow him, we might find Larryboy."

"Wouldn't that be dangerous?" asked Renee.

"I'm not sure about this," said Percy, nervously.

"I'm with you, Junior," said Laura, with a determined look.

"If we don't want to lose him, we have to go *now*," Junior said. Junior jumped onto his sled. **SWOOSH!** He sailed down the hill, in pursuit of Frostbite.

"Let's go!" Laura yelled as she jumped onto her toboggan. Percy and Renee followed on their snowboards.

"Wheee!" shouted Renee.

"Shush!" shushed Laura.

"Sorry," whispered Renee, before letting out one last little "Whee!"

CHAPTER 17

STICKY SITUATION

"Larryboy?
Can you hear me?" Archibald
was speaking through the radio in
Larryboy's suit.
"Larryboy, can you hear me?"
"Althred, ith thad you?"
"Larryboy, I'm having trouble understanding
you. Did you stick your tongue to the ice bars
again?"
"He double dared me," Larryboy said.
"Haven't you learned your lesson about that? You
have to stop taking their dares," Archibald told him.
"Listen, I am working on a plan to defeat Iceberg. I
need you to be patient."
"I'll be bathiend," Larryboy mumbled.
"Who are you talking to?" Snowflake asked as he
came over to the cage.
"No one," said Larryboy.
"No one what?" asked Archibald.
"I'b na dalging do anyone," said Larryboy.
"Good, 'cause I don't want any trouble from
you," said Snowflake. "Iceberg left me in charge
when he and the boys went to town."

"Day wend do down?" asked Larryboy.

"Who went to town?" asked Archibald.

"Arthy, I'm buthy," slurred Larryboy.

"Oh, sorry," said the butler. "I'll call back later."

"What did you say?" said Snowflake.

"Day wend do down?" repeated Larryboy.

"Yes," said Snowflake, "to send off a letter to Iceberg's father. He is the Snow King, you know—a very powerful supervillain."

"Da No King?"

"That's right."

DING-DONG. They were interrupted as the doorbell to the secret hideout rang.

"That's funny," said Snowflake. "My pizza shouldn't be here for another half an hour." Snowflake left the room to answer the door.

"Psst, Larryboy!" Junior and Laura snuck out from behind the door.

"Hetho, Thunior an Wauwa," said Larryboy. "How'd do ged here?"

"We snuck in the back. Renee and Percy are distracting Snowflake at the front door," said Laura. "We don't have much time. We have to get you out of here."

"Bud I'm thuck," said Larryboy.

"I've got just the thing," said Junior. "We can use the hot chocolate I brought for a snack."

The small asparagus opened a thermos and poured some of the hot chocolate onto Larryboy's tongue.

The superhero pulled himself free. "Thanks," he said. "Freedom tastes good!"

"And now the lock," said Junior. He poured the remaining cocoa on the lock of the ice cage. The lock melted, and Larryboy hopped out of the cage.

"What are you kids doing here?" asked the superhero.

"We had to help," said Laura. "This is all our fault. We kids helped Iceberg turn Bumblyburg into an ice world."

"Why would you do that?" Larryboy asked.

"We wanted a snow day, so we wouldn't have to go to school," said Junior. "But we've learned our lesson."

"Yeah, we actually *miss* school," admitted Laura. "Some of it, anyway."

"Really?" asked Larryboy.

"Yeah," said Junior. "My dad was right: when you stop learning, you stop growing."

"Hey!" said Larryboy. "That reminds me of something. My teacher at school talked about the Snow King."

"Who's the Snow King?" the kids asked in unison.

"He was a supervillain that Bok Choy defeated. And he's Iceberg's dad!"

"Really?" asked Junior.

"Bok Choy told us how he defeated the Snow King. Maybe we can defeat Iceberg in the same way."

"What did your teacher say?" asked Laura.

"He said...he said..." stammered Larryboy. "I don't know what he said. I wasn't paying attention."

"Let's find Bok Choy and ask him," said Junior.

"Good idea," said Larryboy.

"Quick," said Laura. "Let's go out the back way before Snowflake returns."

The trio quickly raced out the back. And not a moment too soon! Snowflake walked into the room, carrying a small box.

"Guess what," he said. "That wasn't my pizza at all. But I did manage to buy a box of Veggie Scout cookies. Do you like thick mints?"

Snowflake looked at the empty cage. "Oh, no! Larryboy is gone!" Snowflake looked around the room.

"That can mean only one thing," he said. "More cookies for me!"

CHAPTER 18

BACK TO SCHOOL

"And that is why, class, we need to be humble heroes," Bok Choy lectured a young group of superheroes. Unlike the Bumblyburg Elementary School, the superhero college was still in session.

Suddenly the door burst open, and Larryboy hopped in. "Emergency, Professor Choy!" yelled Larryboy.

"Speaking of humble heroes," Bok Choy said calmly. "Class, let me introduce you to Larryboy."

"Hello, Mr. Larryboy!" recited the class in unison.

"Now then," said Bok Choy. "What is your emergency?"

"Iceberg has turned all of Bumblyburg into ice," said Larryboy. "We must stop him!"

"And why are you telling me?" asked the teacher.

"Well," said Larryboy, "the Snow King is Iceberg's father. And since you defeated the Snow King, I thought you might be able to tell me how I could defeat Iceberg."

"I see," said Bok Choy. "You want me to teach you about the Snow King?"

"Sure," said the superhero.

"Wasn't my last lecture all about the Snow King?"

"Uhm," stuttered the cucumber. "Yeah, but..."

"But you weren't paying attention," frowned Bok Choy. "Maybe this time you will."

Bok Choy went to the front of the room. He drew on the chalkboard for a moment. When he stepped back, he showed the class a complex diagram.

"Now then," he said. "When the Snow King tried to turn Bumblyburg into a frozen wasteland, he used a K.w.a.c.k." Bok Choy pointed to a box on the board.

"A kwack?" asked Larryboy. "Quick, what's a kwack?"

"A King-sized Winterizing Auto-Compression Kalvinator. It's a large freezing machine."

"Got it," said Larryboy. "Are we done?"

"Not hardly," said his teacher. "The K.w.a.c.k. was connected to a hundred different Mini-Hoohas, which he had installed in the sewer system."

"Minihaha?"

"Mini-Hooha," Bok Choy responded. "Miniature Heat Oscillation Obfuscating Hydro-freon Accelerator."

"Oh," said Larryboy. "One of those. I'm running out of time. Can you just tell me how to stop Iceberg?"

"I am teaching you about Iceberg's methods," said the wise professor. "It is through learning that you will find the solution."

"But it's not time for *my* class," said Larryboy. "Can't

we just jump to the answer?"

"Learning requires much more than simply obtaining answers," said Bok Choy. "It is also about wisdom. Whether you are in the classroom or in life, whether you are young or old, when you stop learning—you stop growing. Larryboy, can you tell me what the superhero handbook says in section 20, paragraph 9, subsection 9?"

Larryboy shrugged his shoulders. Bok Choy turned to the students in the classroom.

"Class?" he asked.

The students all spoke in unison. "Instruct a wise man and he will be wiser still; teach a righteous man and he will add to his learning," they chanted.

"That's right," said the teacher. "Larryboy, listen, learn, and grow. It's all part of becoming wiser."

Bok Choy turned back to the diagram on the chalkboard.

"Now then, where was I?" he asked. "Ah, yes. Snow King had each of these Mini-Hoohas wired to the K.w.a.c.k. machine. And when the K.w.a.c.k. was turned on, it pumped out compressed F.r.i.s.b.e.e.s. to each Mini-Hooha. F.r.i.s.b.e.e.s. was Snow King's special creation, a super freezing liquid called Freon Reactivated Ionizing Sodium Bicarbonate Energy Evaporation Solution. Understand?"

"Understand what?" asked Larryboy, looking up in surprise. "Yes. Hoohas. Frisbees. Cold."

"Right."

"So how did you stop the Snow King?" the cucumber asked.

"Simple," said Bok Choy. "I turned off the K.w.a.c.k."

"Simple!" said Larryboy. After a pause, Larryboy asked sheepishly, "Where do I find the k.w.a.c.k. again?"

Bok Choy sighed. "It takes tremendous power to make all the machines work," said Bok Choy. "Such power will give off readings on the Energy Spectrograph. Simply find a large energy drain. That should lead you to the K.w.a.c.k. machine."

"Got it!" Larryboy hopped out of the room. Seconds later, he popped his head back in.

"And thanks! This whole learning thing seems like a pretty good idea," he admitted. Then he was gone.

CHAPTER 19

A NEW LARRYTOY

Larryboy
hurried out into the school
parking lot. Junior, Laura, Percy, and
Renee were waiting for him.

"Hey, kids," Larryboy yelled, "I figured out
what we need to do."

"Larryboy, look at this!" Junior shouted.

Larryboy looked out into the parking lot where
Archibald, his butler, stood among the kids.

"Hey, Archie, what are you doing here?"

In answer, Archie simply pointed. There sat the
Larrymobile. But not the usual Larrymobile. Instead, it
was the Larry*snow*mobile! The car had been converted
to a snowmobile, with treads in the place of the back
wheels and skis up front.

"Cool!" said Larryboy, his eyes sparkling.

"I thought this might help," said Archie. "I also
have a new uniform for you." Archibald brandished a
snowsuit version of the Larryboy costume. "It's
insulated to keep you warm. And it has traction
grips to keep you from falling on the ice."

"Nifty! Thanks," Larryboy said. He grabbed
the new suit and jumped inside it.

"Wait," said Archibald. "There are a few more features..."

"I don't have time to learn about new features," said Larryboy, his face set in determination.

"You don't have *time* to learn?" Archibald cocked his eyebrow. "Where have I heard that before?"

"I have to quickly find Iceberg's kwack doodad and the Frisbee juice, so I can turn it off," explained the cucumber.

"Kwack doodad?" asked Junior.

"Frisbee juice?" questioned Laura.

The kids leaned forward in excitement.

"Yep," said the superhero. "Bok Choy said that the kwack thingy uses a lot of energy. And that energy drain should show up on an Energy Spectacle-something."

"Do you mean an Energy Spectrograph?" asked Archibald.

"That's exactly right," said Larryboy with surprise.

"I have one of those in the Larrycave," said the butler.

"Great, then off we go to the Larrycave! I'm outta here!" Larryboy revved up the Larrysnowmobile and zoomed off.

"Larryboy, wait!" called Archibald. But it was too late. Larryboy was gone. "Oh, my."

"Let's follow him," said Junior. "He still might need our help."

The other kids agreed.

"Say, Master Junior?" asked Archibald.

"Yes, sir?"

"I don't suppose you could give me a lift?"

"Sure, hop on," the youngster said.

Archibald slipped onto the back of Junior's sled, and they slid off down the hill.

CHAPTER 20

OF SNOWBALLS AND SNOW PEAS

"There it is!" said Larryboy.

Larryboy and the kids crouched on a hill, looking down at an igloo. Frostbite, Avalanche, and Snowflake stood outside.

"Archie says the Spector-thingymabob indicated this is the spot," said Larryboy.

"I bet the snow peas are guarding the K.w.a.c.k. machine," said Junior.

"Hmmm." Larryboy thought for a moment. "I'll need a distraction to get inside."

"We've got just the thing," said Laura. "Ready, kids?"

"Ready!"

The foursome jumped on their sled, toboggan, and snowboards and zoomed down the hill. Each had a pile of snowballs.

"Hey, pea pods!" Junior yelled. "Snowball fight!"

The kids pelted the villains with snowballs as they zoomed past and continued down the hill past the igloo.

"What do those kids think they are doing?" snarled Frostbite.

"I'll teach them," growled Avalanche.

"Snowball fight? Cool!" said Snowflake.

The three snow peas fired up their jet-skates and took off after the kids. As soon as they were gone, Larryboy zoomed up in his Larrysnowmobile, hopped out and quickly entered the igloo.

CHAPTER 21

OFF KILTER

It wasn't too hard to
locate the King-sized Winterizing
Auto-Compression Kalvinator. A large
machine stood in the middle of the room.
Red, yellow, and blue lights blinked all over
the machine like a Christmas tree gone mad. On
top of the contraption, sparks jumped between two
antennae, making a loud **ZAP** with each spark. The
contraption roared and groaned and clunked, making
an incredible racket.

"Hmmm," said Larryboy. "I wonder how you turn
this thing off."

Then he noticed a big switch on the side of the
machine. The switch was labeled On and Off. It was
currently in the On position.

"No, too easy," said Larryboy. "But it can't hurt to try."
Larryboy pulled the switch to Off. Slowly, the
roars, groans, and clunks ground to a halt. The yellow lights stopped blinking, then the red, and then
the blue. The antennae at the top of the machine
threw a final spark, and the last **ZAP** echoed in
the room. The machine was off!

"I did it," he said. "I did it! I did it!"

Larryboy ran out of the igloo.

"I did it! We've won! We've..." That's when Larryboy noticed that the ice was still there.

"Hey, if I turned off the doodad, why isn't the ice melting?"

"I'm glad you asked," smiled Iceberg.

Larryboy spun around. Iceberg sat in his plastic bowl just behind the hero.

"Hey, I learned how to defeat you!" shouted Larryboy.

"You learned how to defeat my father," Iceberg corrected.

"It will work on you too," said Larryboy. "Won't it?"

"Not if I have learned more about my father's failure than you have," said the head of lettuce. "*He* was defeated when his K.w.a.c.k. was turned off. So I made a few changes. Once the K.w.a.c.k. feeds F.r.i.s.b.e.e.s. to my Mini-Hoohas, they are able to keep freezing for a long time. Time enough for me to turn the K.w.a.c.k. on again."

"Not if I put you in jail first!" Larryboy warned, turning his head to the side.

POP! Larryboy hurled one of his plunger ears toward Iceberg. But before it could hit, Frostbite moved in front of him! **PLOP!** The plunger stuck to Frostbite.

"Fool," said Iceberg. "You didn't think those children could distract my team for long, did you?"

Larryboy followed Iceberg's gaze. Avalanche and Snowflake stood beside Junior, Laura, Renee, and Percy. The kids were tied up!

"Take care of him, gentlemen," Iceberg commanded. "And then take care of those annoying children!"

Frostbite, Avalanche, and Snowflake looked menacingly at Larryboy.

"Uh-oh," said Larryboy.

CHAPTER 22

WHIPLASH!

"Want to go for a ride?" Frostbite asked. "Come on, boys!"

The three snow peas hooked up and zoomed off together. They pulled Larryboy behind them; faster and faster they went. Then **WHOOSH!** The trio came to a sudden stop. Larryboy was whipped past them and hurtled toward a snow bank!

Hmmm, thought our hero. *This is like déjà vu all over again.*

"Larryboy, come in Larryboy," Archibald was calling on Larryboy's helmet radio.

"I'm a little busy, Archie," said Larryboy. "I'm being whiplashed."

"Then use your snow-brake!"

"What snow-brake?"

"The one I installed in your new costume. Turn your head to the right twice."

Larryboy tried turning his head, but he was so dizzy from being whiplashed that he didn't know his right from his left! Suddenly, he heard music and singing.

"*He's bigger than Godzilla or the monsters on TV. Oh...*"

"Alfred!" screeched Larryboy.

"The *right,* Master Larry, the *right!*" Alfred shouted. "Turning your head to the left turns on the radio."

Larryboy turned his head the other direction twice. A metal claw popped out of the back of his costume and dug into the ice. Larryboy came to an immediate stop.

"Cool," said the hero. "And now it's the snow peas' turn!" Larryboy twisted his body around. The rope on the plunger ear became taut.

"Uh-oh," said Frostbite, as he was pulled backward. Avalanche and Snowflake, still attached to Frostbite, were also being pulled backward.

"How about doing circles, boys!" Larryboy taunted. Using his brake as traction, the hero spun in a circle. At the other end of the rope, the three snow peas slid round and round as Larryboy made them go faster and faster.

"Now it's time for a ride!" **POP!** Larryboy released the plunger ear. The three snow peas flew off, skating out of control.

BAM! Frostbite smashed into a snowdrift.

BAM! Avalanche smashed into Frostbite.

"Look out, I'm going to... Oh never mind!" shouted Snowflake as—**BAM!**—he smashed into the other two. The three lay in a heap on the snowdrift.

"Now it's *your* turn, Iceberg," Larryboy said, turning to Iceberg. **POP!** Larryboy sent his ear toward the villain.

PLOP! It stuck right to Iceberg's container!

"Try getting out of this one," said Larryboy.

"OK," said Iceberg, as his container began to hum.

"What's that?" asked Larryboy.

"Oh, I have a few tricks of my own," boasted the head of lettuce. "My bowl comes with its own Mini-Hooha. Right now I am supercooling the air around me!"

Larryboy noticed that his plunger ear had frosted over. **CRACK!** The plunger shattered into pieces.

"You see," said the villain, "anything that I get close to will freeze and shatter. Watch as I get closer to *you*."

A series of jet rockets attached to the villain's bowl roared to life. The bowl rose into the air as cold air swirled about him. Using the jets, Iceberg zoomed toward Larryboy. As he came closer, the rope that ran to the plunger frosted over and splintered into pieces.

"Peanut brittle!" said Larryboy.

"No...ice brittle..." said the villain, as Iceberg hovered closer and closer.

CHAPTER 23

ICEBERG OFF THE STARBOARD BOW

Larryboy
could feel the air getting colder
as Iceberg approached.

"Look!" he shouted. "A salad shooter!"

"Where?" Iceberg shrieked as he turned
to look.

"Made you look," mocked Larryboy. He raced
around Iceberg and dove for the Larrysnowmobile.

"Oh, no you don't," threatened Iceberg.

He raced after Larryboy. But before he could
catch up, our hero jumped into his vehicle, fired up
the engine, and drove off in his Larrysnowmobile.

"Whew," he said. "That was close!" But glancing
into his rearview mirror, Larryboy could see that
Iceberg was right behind him! Larryboy sped up, but
Iceberg's rockets were powerful. The head of lettuce
was right on his tail! Our hero banked left and headed
across a field.

"Archie! Archie, are you there?"

The videophone came to life. Archibald
looked out at our hero. "Did the snow-brake
work?" he asked.

"Yeah, but nothing else has," said Larryboy.

"I turned off the k.w.a.c.k. doodad, but the ice didn't melt. And now Iceberg is on my tail. He's going to freeze me!"

"Well, that *is* a quandary," said Archibald. "Did Bok Choy teach you anything else about Snow King and Iceberg?"

"Well, he was showing me all sorts of stuff," said Larryboy. "But I wasn't paying attention. I only wanted a quick answer."

"Oh, my," said Archibald.

"Why didn't I pay attention? Professor Choy told me that learning was about much more than answers. He told me that if I stopped learning, I'd stop growing. And now I won't ever grow in wisdom again! What kind of superhero have I become?"

"Maybe it isn't all hopeless," said Archibald. "Can you remember *anything* he said at all?"

"Well," said the cucumber. "He had a diagram on the board. It had the K.w.a.c.k. on it."

"What else was on the diagram?"

"Oh, lots of stuff," replied Larryboy. "It was very pretty."

Archibald tried to keep his voice from showing his rising distress. "Can you remember anything *specific* about the diagram?" he asked.

"Yes!" said the hero triumphantly. "Some of it was blue!"

"I mean, anything specific about what he drew!"

"Oh, that," said Larryboy. "Let me think. Oh, yeah. He said the Snow King planted minithingies in the sewer. That's how everything got so cold. **YIKES!**"

Larryboy was heading straight for a tree! He banked

sharply to the right, nearly causing the snowmobile to topple over. Larryboy leaned hard to the left, and the snowmobile plopped back upright.

Larryboy checked his mirror. As Iceberg passed the tree, it froze over and shattered.

"Iceberg is still right behind me," he reported. "If he gets too close to me, I'm an instant veggiesicle."

"Oh, dear," said Archibald. "I'm out of ideas."

"Wait!" said Larryboy. "I'm not. Quick, Archie, check your map of Bumblyburg. I need to find a way into the city's sewer."

Larryboy checked his rearview mirror again. Iceberg was gaining on him! Icicles popped in the air around him. Larryboy tried to think warm thoughts, but he could feel the air around him growing colder. His plan had to work!

CHAPTER 24

FIFTEEN DEGREES BELOW STREET LEVEL

"Take a left at that tree, Larryboy."

The superhero banked left and zoomed across the field.

"Straight ahead," continued Archibald. "You should see a large pipe. That will get you into the sewer."

"Good job, Archie!" said Larryboy. "Now, keep an eye on the map. You have to make sure I go into every tunnel."

Larryboy zoomed toward the large pipe, but Iceberg was right behind him as the Larrysnowmobile entered the sewer.

"Aagh! I've gone blind," screamed the hero.

"No, you haven't," Archibald reassured him. "It's dark in the tunnels. Turn on your headlights."

Larryboy pushed the white button, and his windshield wipers came to life.

"The green button, Larryboy," said Archibald. "Remember,

lime for lights. White for wipers!"

"Right," said Larryboy, as he hit the green button and his headlights came on. **"AAAAHHH!"** he shrieked. He was heading straight for a wall!

"Right! Turn right!" Archibald yelled.

Larryboy swerved right and checked his mirror. He could barely see Iceberg rocketing along, the walls freezing as he passed.

"Take the next left," Archibald said as Larryboy swerved. "Now right and then left again."

Larryboy swerved through the tunnels. Each time he turned, Iceberg turned with him, turn after turn after turn.

"That's it," said Archibald. "Now you just have to... Look out!"

"I have to what?" asked Larryboy. He peered out his front windshield and saw that he was headed straight for another wall! Larryboy slammed on his brakes, and Iceberg skidded to a halt behind him.

"Archie, it's a dead end," Larryboy whispered urgently. "I'm trapped."

"There's a manhole cover above you, leading up to the street," said Archibald.

Larryboy hopped out and stood on top of the Larrysnowmobile. He looked up and saw the manhole cover. But Iceberg was standing right under it!

"There's no escaping now," said Iceberg. "It's time for cucumber ice cream!"

"Not so fast," Larryboy said with a smile. "Hear anything?"

DRIP. DRIP. DRIP. The sound echoed throughout the

sewer.

"What's that?" Iceberg asked.

"That is the ice above us melting," said our hero. "Your minithingamabobs have been destroyed."

"My Mini-Hoohas?" Iceberg looked behind him. He could see pieces of the shattered machines lining the floor.

"But...how?" was all he could manage to sputter.

"*You* did it," said Larryboy. "You supercooled everything you came near. While you chased me, I lead you past every minidoohickey you put in the sewer. As you passed them, they shattered to pieces."

"You may have destroyed my Mini-Hoohas," said Iceberg, "but I can still destroy *you!*"

"Maybe," said Larryboy. "But right now there is a ton of water directly above you. And only that metal cover stands between you and the water."

Iceberg looked up at the manhole cover. It was frosted over.

"Looks brittle, doesn't it?" asked Larryboy.

"**ARRGH!**" yelled Iceberg as he lurched toward the cucumber.

POP! Larryboy shot his remaining plunger ear. It smashed into the manhole cover, and the cover shattered! A flood of water poured down on Iceberg, instantly freezing, which trapped Iceberg in a giant icicle!

"**WHEW,**" said Larryboy. "That was close. Now to get the police to help me defrost this Iceberg!"

CHAPTER 25

THE ICEBERG GOETH

Slam!

Officer Olaf closed the door on the paddy wagon. Inside was a soggy Iceberg, looking rather wilted inside his bowl. At his side sat Frostbite, Avalanche, and Snowflake. Only Snowflake looked excited to be there.

"Play the siren, play the siren!" the large snow pea chanted, as the paddy wagon rode off toward the Bumblyburg jail.

"Thanks, Larryboy," Officer Olaf said. "Bumblyburg would still be Bumbly-*Ice*-burg if it hadn't been for you."

"Well, if I hadn't learned my lesson that learning is a good idea, I'd be a frozen veggie pop. Then my tongue would stick to my lips all the time. But Bok Choy was right; you're never too old to keep learning. When you stop learning, you stop growing."

"Sounds like a wise teacher," said Croswell.

"The kids helped, too," said Larryboy. "I hope their parents go easy on them." Junior, Laura, Percy, and Renee stood a few feet away with their parents, making explanations. They were shaking in their boots—and this time not from the cold.

"And that's the whole story," said Junior. "We're really sorry."

"Yeah," said Laura. "We sure learned our lesson."

"And what did you learn about playing with the sink?" asked Percy's dad.

"Never, ever plug the drain and leave the water running," Percy repeated.

"Not only did it cause a lot of damage to the house," said Junior, "it's also very dangerous."

"We'll never do it again," said Renee.

"So that's that, right?" asked Percy.

"Not quite," said Percy's mom.

"You still need to be punished for flooding Bumblyburg," said Mr. Asparagus. "We parents have agreed that you are to be suspended for one week."

"For one week," explained Laura's mom, "you can't go to school."

"Can't go to school!" yelled Junior. "That's not fair! We've already lost a week of school."

"Yeah," said Renee. "We miss art and writing."

"And gym and reading," complained Percy.

"And math," added Laura.

"So, you *like* school?" asked Mr. Asparagus.

"Well, sort of," said Junior, embarrassed to admit it.

"A little," said Laura, looking down at her shoes.

"In a way," said Percy. "Sometimes."

"Oui," whispered Renee.

"I see," said Mr. Asparagus, looking at the other parents. They all were smiling. "The punishment is a week of no school. And since you've already missed school, then you've already been punished."

"Really?" asked Junior. "Thanks, Dad."

"Yeah, thanks," said Laura.

"Oui," whispered Renee.

"Looks like my work here is done," said Larryboy. He hopped to the manhole opening and looked down. "Hey, the sewer is flooded!"

"Of course," Chief Croswell said. "Where did you think all the water would go?"

"Well," Larryboy said, "I didn't think that far ahead. I sort of left my Larrysnowmobile parked down there."

"Oh, don't worry. The water will clear out before long."

"How long?"

"About a week."

"A week?" said Larryboy. "I wonder how I'll explain this to Archie."

Larryboy hopped down the street, talking to himself. "Hey, Archie, guess what? You know how you always tell me to take the Larrymobile to the carwash? No, that won't work. Hey, Archie, you know how you keep telling me that walking is good exercise? No, he won't go for that either. Hey, Archie, you know how hard it is to find a parking space downtown? Well, not anymore. No, that's not going to do it. Hey, Archie, you know how I always wanted a Larrysubmarine? Yeah! That one's perfect."

Larryboy's voice trailed off as he disappeared into the distance.

THE END

OWN THE ENTIRE COLLECTION OF LARRYBOY BOOKS AND DVDS!

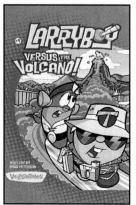

LarryBoy Versus the Volcano!
Softcover 978-0-310-70728-8

The Good, the Bad and the Eggly
LarryBoy Cartoon DVD

BOOKS

LarryBoy and the Emperor of Envy (Book 1)
Softcover 978-0-310-70467-6

LarryBoy and the Awful Ear Wacks Attacks (Book 2)
Softcover 978-0-310-70468-3

LarryBoy and the Sinister Snow Day (Book 3)
Softcover 978-0-310-70561-1

LarryBoy and the Yodelnapper (Book 4)
Softcover 978-0-310-70562-8

LarryBoy and the Good, the Bad, and the Eggly (Book 5)
Softcover 978-0-310-70650-2

LarryBoy in the Attack of Outback Jack (Book 6)
Softcover 978-0-310-70649-6

LarryBoy and the Amazing Brain-Twister (Book 7)
Softcover 978-0-310-70651-9

LarryBoy and the Abominable Trashman (Book 8)
Softcover 978-0-310-70652-6

LarryBoy Versus the Volcano (Book 9)
Softcover 978-0-310-70728-8

LarryBoy and the Snowball of Doom (Book 10)
Softcover 978-0-310-70729-5

DVDS

The Angry Eyebrows
LarryBoy Cartoon DVD

Leggo My Ego
LarryBoy Cartoon DVD

The Yodelnapper
LarryBoy Cartoon DVD

The Good, the Bad, and the Eggly
LarryBoy Cartoon DVD

LarryBoy and the Rumor Weed
VeggieTales DVD

LarryBoy & the Fib from Outer Space
VeggieTales DVD

LarryBoy and the Bad Apple
VeggieTales DVD

CPSIA information can be obtained at www.ICGtesting.com
Printed in the USA
LVOW040941041012

301481LV00001B/1/P